WITHDRAWN

TEEN STRONG

Center Stage WITH

Millie Bobby Brown

by Heather DiLorenzo Williams

For Lauren, *who stood up for what she believed in with passion and strength.*

Millie Bobby Brown
TEEN STRONG

Copyright © 2022
Published by Full Tilt Press
Written by Heather DiLorenzo Williams
All rights reserved.

Printed in the United States of America.
No part of this book may be reproduced in any manner whatsoever without written permission, except in the case of brief quotations embodied in critical articles and reviews.
All websites that appear in the back matter were correct and functioning when this book was sent to press.

Full Tilt Press
42964 Osgood Road
Fremont, CA 94539
readfulltilt.com

Full Tilt Press publications may be purchased for educational, business, or sales promotional use.

Editorial Credits
Design and layout by Sara Radka
Edited by Meghan Gottschall

Image Credits
Alamy: The Hollywood Archive/PictureLux, 4, The Hollywood Archive/PictureLux, 26 (bottom); Getty Images: Alberto E. Rodriguez, 11, Dimitrios Kambouris, 3, Fox Photos, 16, Frazer Harrison, 22, 27 (top), Frederick M. Brown, 8, 26 (top), Jacopo Raule, 7, Jamie McCarthy, cover, 1, Kevin Winter, 14, 15, 24, 27 (bottom), Michael Loccisano, 10, Mike Coppola, 20, Netflix/Charley Gallay, 12, Nicholas Hunt, 21, TNT/John Sciulli, 6, UNICEF/Monica Schipper, 18, 29, background; Newscom: Album/Daniel McFadden/Wanda Qingdao Studioes/Warner Bros./Legendary Pictures, 23, Cover Images, 17, MEGA/converse.com, 19, MEGA/Courtesy of UEFA, 25 (top), United Archives/Impress, 13, Warner Bros/PCMA Prod/Legendary Entertainment/Netflix, 25 (bottom); Shutterstock: aniok, background; Wikimedia: Nojo13, 9

ISBN: 978-1-62920-905-0 (library binding)
ISBN: 978-1-62920-909-8 (ePub)

CONTENTS

Introduction 4
Getting Started 6
Becoming Teen Strong 10
Inspiration 14
Work in Progress 18
A Bright Future 22
Timeline 26
Quiz 28
Activity 29
Glossary 30
Read More 31
Internet Sites 31
Index 32

Introduction

Although she did not have much to say at first, Eleven's intense stare spoke volumes during season 1 of Stranger Things.

Twelve-year-old Millie Bobby Brown sits in a chair surrounded by mirrors and people. Behind her, the *Stranger Things* stylist cuts off large chunks of Millie's long hair. Then she shaves Millie's head. Eleven—the character that will launch Millie's career—appears in the mirror. Millie giggles. Then she turns to the camera and gives Eleven's **fierce** glare.

"The day I shaved my head was the most **empowering** moment of my whole life," Millie later wrote on Instagram. She had always hidden behind her long hair. That day, Millie realized that hair is not what makes someone beautiful. True beauty and strength come from within. She decided to make it her mission to share this message with other teen girls. Millie soon became one of the world's most recognized young actresses. She used her voice to make a difference in the lives of kids and teens everywhere.

....

fierce: very strong or intense
empower: to give a feeling of power or confidence

MILLIE BOBBY BROWN

Getting Started

Millie's parents are Kelly and Robert Brown. Their support made it possible for her to pursue a career in acting.

Millie Bobby Brown was born in southern Spain on February 19, 2004. She is one of four children. She has two sisters and a brother. Her parents are from England. The family moved back there when Millie was four years old.

Millie is deaf in one ear. Despite this, she is a talented singer and loves music. She started doing Amy Winehouse **impersonations** when she was about four. She also loves rap music. Cardi B and Nikki Minaj are her favorite rappers.

Millie's early love of performing was not limited to music. She decided she wanted to become an actress when she was around eight years old. She had never been on stage or taken an acting class. When her family moved to Florida in 2012, Millie started taking acting classes. Then they moved to Los Angeles so she could follow her dream of becoming an actress.

Nikki Minaj is known for her unique style, which sometimes includes brightly colored clothing, creative nails and makeup, and a variety of wigs.

For exercise, Millie enjoys boxing. She trains every day.

impersonation: acting or sounding like another person

Millie got her first role in a television show when she was just nine years old.

Millie's Beginning

Millie started going to **auditions** right after her family moved to Florida. She learned how to do an American accent from watching the Disney Channel. But her career did not take off at first. She got a few guest roles on shows such as *Grey's Anatomy* and *Modern Family*. Then she auditioned for a movie. She did not get the part. Millie thought about giving up on acting. But she didn't. She was determined to become an actress. "Once I find something I want to do, nobody's stopping me," she told *Variety*.

audition: a tryout performance for an actor or musician

Millie's luck changed in 2015. She auditioned for a new Netflix show called *Stranger Things*. It was set in the 1980s. Most of the main characters were kids. The director and the show's creators loved Millie's audition. She got the part. *Stranger Things* became a hit. Before long, Millie Bobby Brown was famous.

THE MONTAUK PROJECT

Stranger Things is based on a real-life government experiment called the Montauk Project. The project was housed at an air force base in Montauk, New York. According to rumors, the United States government was conducting experiments in time travel, **teleportation**, and mind control using human subjects. Many of the experiments in Stranger Things were based on the accounts of a man who says he was one of the subjects of the Montauk Project.

Montauk Air Force Station

teleportation: disappearing from one place and appearing in another

Becoming Teen Strong

Thanks to Stranger Things, Millie and her co-stars (from left to right, Gaten Matarazzo, Natalia Dyer, Noah Schnapp, Caleb McLaughlin, and Finn Wolfhard) are some of the most recognizable teen stars in the world.

Millie was 11 when she got the role of Eleven in *Stranger Things*. The part was challenging. But it was no match for Millie's talent. Eleven is very important to the events of the first season. However, she only says around 250 words over the eight episodes! Millie had to rely on facial expressions and body language. She met this challenge head-on.

The show's writers and directors say Millie nailed Eleven's **signature** glare in her audition. That is why they gave her the part. Eleven has many special abilities and strong emotions. Millie mastered them all. She also did many of her own stunts.

One of Millie's first awards was Best Actor at the 2017 MTV Movie and TV Awards, where she was also nominated for "Best Hero."

Millie has been **nominated** for more than 40 awards. She has won 17, including the People's Choice Award for Favorite Female TV Star.

signature: a distinctive mark or characteristic

nominate: to name someone as a candidate for an award

MILLIE BOBBY BROWN 11

The Duffer Brothers, Ross and Matt (second and third from left), created Stranger Things. They are twins and have been making movies together since they were in third grade.

Big Ideas

In 2022, *Stranger Things* began its fourth season. Eleven was still in the middle of the action. Some of the show's most important scenes involve Millie. The directors say they have never given her a task she could not perform. "It's like a singer who can hit any note. Her range is just absolutely incredible," they told *Variety*. The show's writers created Eleven long before they met Millie. But they can be even more creative with the character because she is such a good actress.

The entertainment world has taken notice of Millie's work on *Stranger Things*. She has been nominated for two Emmy Awards for her role as Eleven. She is one of the youngest nominees in Emmys history. But to Millie, the show's biggest reward is her friendships with the cast. Her on-screen friends are some of her real-life besties. She received MTV's first-ever Best Actor award in 2017. As she accepted it, she called the cast her second family.

STAND BY ME

Stranger Things is set in the '80s. Millie's favorite '80s movie is *Stand By Me*. She loves it because of the close friendships between the characters. Her *Stranger Things* co-stars are some of her best friends. They often go to movies and theme parks together.

Stand By Me is based on a **novella** called *The Body*. It was written by well-known horror writer Stephen King. *Stranger Things* contains many references to his books. Like *Stand By Me*, *Stranger Things* is about a group of best friends who band together against bullies and other problems.

novella: a work of fiction that is longer than a short story but shorter than a standard novel

Inspiration

Millie is completely comfortable in front of the camera, whether she is on the set of *Stranger Things*, or goofing off at an awards show. She hopes to inspire her fans to feel comfortable being themselves too.

Millie wants to keep her life as simple as possible. Most actors live in Hollywood or New York City. But Millie splits her time between London, England, and Atlanta, Georgia. She told *Variety* magazine that she likes Georgia because it is "calm, peaceful, beautiful." *Stranger Things* is filmed in Atlanta. Living there also allows her to be close to her family.

Millie also wants to enjoy her childhood for as long as she can. She does not want to rush into **adulthood**. She likes having fun. Spending time with her dogs and pet tortoises makes her happy. She also loves playing jokes on her fellow cast members.

Millie says laughing with her co-stars is one of her favorite things about being part of the *Stranger Things* cast.

Millie started her own clean cosmetics line in 2019. It is called florence by mills. Clean cosmetics are non-toxic and contain simple ingredients.

adulthood: the part of life when you are a grown-up

MILLIE BOBBY BROWN 15

Although she was an award-winning actress, Audrey Hepburn retired from filmmaking and dedicated the final years of her life to her family and her work as an activist.

    Being in the spotlight means dealing with negative opinions and mean comments. This happens a lot on social media. Millie does not let that make her feel bad. She has used her voice to encourage others to be comfortable with who they are.

    One of Millie's heroes is Audrey Hepburn. She was an actress and **humanitarian**. She spent time helping poor children all over the world. Hepburn inspired Millie to be an **activist**. She wants to overcome her own obstacles and help others do the same.

humanitarian: someone who cares about the needs of other people

activist: a person who works for social or political change

Millie has experienced bullying in person and online. However, she refuses to let bullying bring her down. She wants to encourage other kids who are bullied to have the same attitude. Millie has also struggled with anxiety. This has made her a more understanding person. She considers it an honor and a responsibility to share her struggles with others.

Millie's work outside of acting includes a line of charms that she designed with Pandora Jewelry. The charms focus on personal style and self-expression.

BULLYING BY THE NUMBERS

160,000 students skip school every year to avoid bullying.

1 in 5 students age 12 to 18 have experienced bullying.

42% of students said their bullying happened in the classroom.

64% of students stay silent and don't report their experience.

https://www.dosomething.org/us/facts/11-facts-about-bullying, 2020
https://www.liahonaacademy.com/2019-shocking-statistics-on-bullying.html, 2019

Work in Progress

Millie is one of many teen activists who are speaking up about issues such as climate change, teenage depression, and bullying.

Millie spends a lot of her free time working as an activist. She has used her fame to speak out on many issues. These include gun violence, bullying, and climate change. Millie was named a UNICEF Goodwill **Ambassador** in 2018. She was also named in *Time* magazine's 100 most influential people in 2018. Millie is the youngest person to have both honors.

Millie has helped design products that promote happiness and self-worth with Converse and Pandora jewelry. She is also a Together #WePlayStrong ambassador for the Union of European Football Associations. This group promotes girls' and women's soccer.

ambassador: someone who represents a country or organization

Millie's 2021 Converse collection, which celebrates self-expression and female empowerment, includes a collaboration with Thai artist Pauline Wattanodom.

On UNICEF World Children's Day in November 2020, Millie talked virtually with three teens from around the world about bullying, COVID-19, and how kids can make the world a better place.

MILLIE BOBBY BROWN 19

Giving Back

Millie's message is the same no matter which organization she is representing. She wants young people around the world to be healthy, safe, and confident. "I will shine a light on issues that **vulnerable** children have suffered around the world," Millie said on the day she became a UNICEF Ambassador. She uses her social media presence to shine that light every day.

As a UNICEF Goodwill Ambassador, Millie encourages young people to speak up and use their voices to change the world.

Millie is determined to make social media a happier, safer space. "Social media is one of the best places in the world and one of the worst," she said in *Glamour* magazine. She calls the negativity on social media a disease. Millie uses her Instagram account to spread love and kindness. She only shares positive messages. She also gives shout-outs to other young activists who inspire her. As of May 2021, more than 45 million people follow her on Instagram.

WHAT IS UNICEF?

UNICEF stands for the United Nations International Children's Fund. It was founded in 1946 to protect the rights of children around the world. UNICEF helps children stay healthy by providing food, vaccinations, and medical care. UNICEF also sponsors programs that help kids in many countries get an education. Celebrity ambassadors help spread the word about UNICEF's programs. Lionel Messi, Shakira, and Millie Bobby Brown are among the organization's many celebrity ambassadors.

vulnerable: in a weak position and likely to be hurt in some way

A Bright Future

Millie's Stranger Things co-star David Harbour says he feels protective of the teen star, claiming that the two of them often argue like father and daughter between scenes.

Millie's acting career is not slowing down. In 2019, she starred in *Godzilla: King of the Monsters*. She also starred in its **sequel**, *Godzilla vs. Kong* in 2021. She and her sister Paige produced a Netflix film based on the Enola Holmes novels. These focus on Sherlock Holmes's younger sister. Millie plays the title character, who finds her voice and learns about female empowerment while she's solving mysteries.

In addition to season 4 of *Stranger Things*, Millie has several projects in the works with Netflix. She is also set to play the main characters in two movies based on novels, *The Girls I've Been* and *The Thing About Jellyfish*.

The *Stranger Things* creators say Millie has a rare understanding of how to move in front of the camera. Her *Stranger Things* co-star David Harbour believes she is **destined** to be one of the greatest actresses of her generation. He compared her to **legendary** actress Meryl Streep.

Millie's role in *Godzilla: King of the Monsters* pits the teenager against a huge lizard, a three-headed monster, and a giant moth.

Millie and her family donated 40,000 meals to food banks in New Mexico and Georgia to help families struggling during the 2020 COVID-19 shutdown.

sequel: a book or movie that continues a story
destined: meant to happen
legendary: famous for accomplishing great things

Teen Strong

Even as her career grows, Millie is determined to stay focused on what is most important to her. "I have learned a lot from Eleven," she said in 2019. "Yes, she's powerful, but she is also a loyal friend and protector."

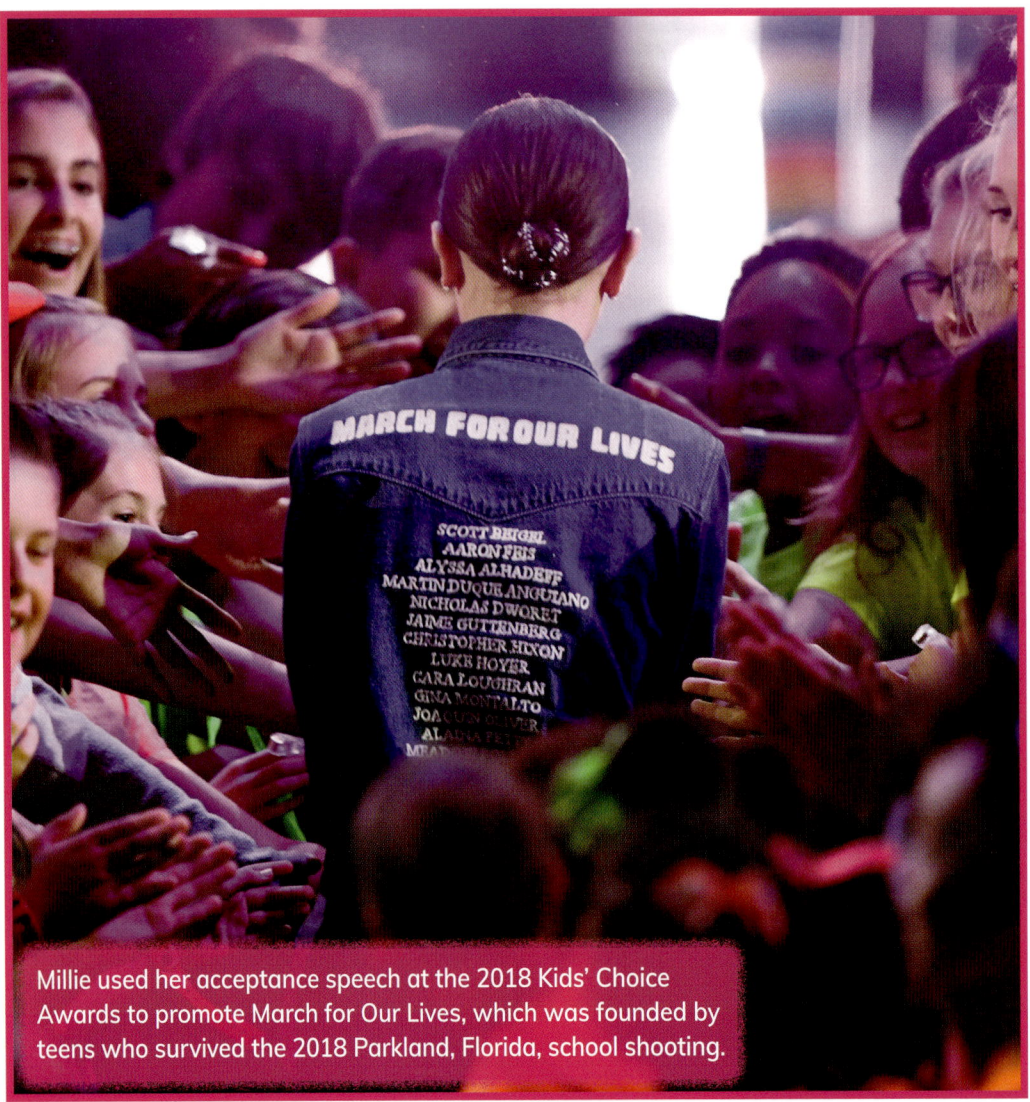

Millie used her acceptance speech at the 2018 Kids' Choice Awards to promote March for Our Lives, which was founded by teens who survived the 2018 Parkland, Florida, school shooting.

Millie continues to work to make positive changes in the world. She celebrated her 16th birthday in a unique way. She posted a video about some of her most painful moments as an actress. She called out the "inappropriate comments . . . and incessant insults" she has dealt with. But Millie went on to say, "Not ever will I be defeated." As she follows in the footsteps of her hero Audrey Hepburn, acting is only half of Millie Bobby Brown's work. The other half is making the world a better place.

A lifelong Liverpool FC fan, Millie hopes her involvement with UEFA's Together #WePlayStrong campaign will encourage teen girls to become more involved in sports.

THE ENOLA HOLMES MYSTERIES

Almost 120 years after the first Sherlock Holmes mystery was written by Sir Arthur Conan Doyle, Nancy Springer wrote about another member of the Holmes family—Sherlock's little sister Enola. The six-novel series follows the bright, independent teenager across London as she attempts to escape her meddling brothers and find her missing mother. Along the way, Enola solves several mysteries of her own, proving that sleuthing is in her blood.

Timeline

February 19, 2004
Millie Bobby Brown is born in Spain.

2012
Millie's family moves to the United States so she can pursue a career in acting.

2013
Millie gets her first acting role as a guest star on *Once Upon a Time in Wonderland*.

2016
Millie is cast as Eleven in the Netflix show *Stranger Things*.